# DEXTER BEXLEY
### AND ### THE # BIG
# BLUE BEASTIE

# JOEL STEWART

PICTURE CORGI

Dexter Bexley scooted . . .

# DEXTER BEXLEY

# IG

## EASTIE

Please return on or before the latest date above.
You can renew online at *www.kent.gov.uk/libs*
or by telephone 08458 247 200

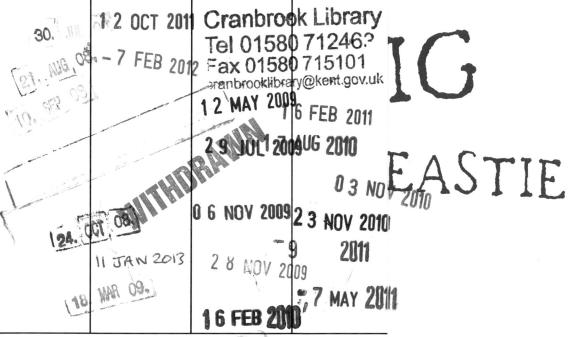

**CHARTER MARK**
CUSTOMER SERVICE EXCELLENCE

**Libraries & Archives**

**Kent County Council**
00884\DTP\RN\07 07   LIB 7

*In memory of Spook,
who knew when to go*

DEXTER BEXLEY AND THE BIG BLUE BEASTIE
A PICTURE CORGI BOOK 978 0 552 55435 0

First published in Great Britain by Doubleday,
an imprint of Random House Children's Books
A Random House Group Company

Doubleday edition published 2007
Picture Corgi edition published 2008

3 5 7 9 10 8 6 4

Copyright © Joel Stewart, 2007

The right of Joel Stewart to be identified as the author and illustrator of this work has been asserted
in accordance with the Copyright, Designs and Patents Act 1988.

Set in Joel 1 Regular

Picture Corgi Books are published by Random House Children's Books,
61–63 Uxbridge Road, London W5 5SA

www.kidsatrandomhouse.co.uk
www.rbooks.co.uk

Addresses for companies within The Random House Group Limited can be found at:
www.randomhouse.co.uk/offices.htm

THE RANDOM HOUSE GROUP Limited Reg. No. 954009

A CIP catalogue record for this book is available from the British Library.

Printed in Singapore

. . . and scooted.

Right into . . .

. . . a Big Blue Beastie!

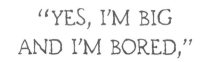

But Dexter Bexley had a much better idea.

"HOLD ON.
I HAVE A
MUCH BETTER IDEA,"

said Dexter Bexley.

Dexter Bexley and the Big Blue Beastie scooted . . .

. . . and scooted, until . . .

# Dexter Bexley and the Big Blue Beastie

went into business

delivering flowers.

Dexter Bexley and the Big Blue Beastie gave up
the flower delivery business and became . . .

# BEXLEY AND BEAST:
## Private Detectives.

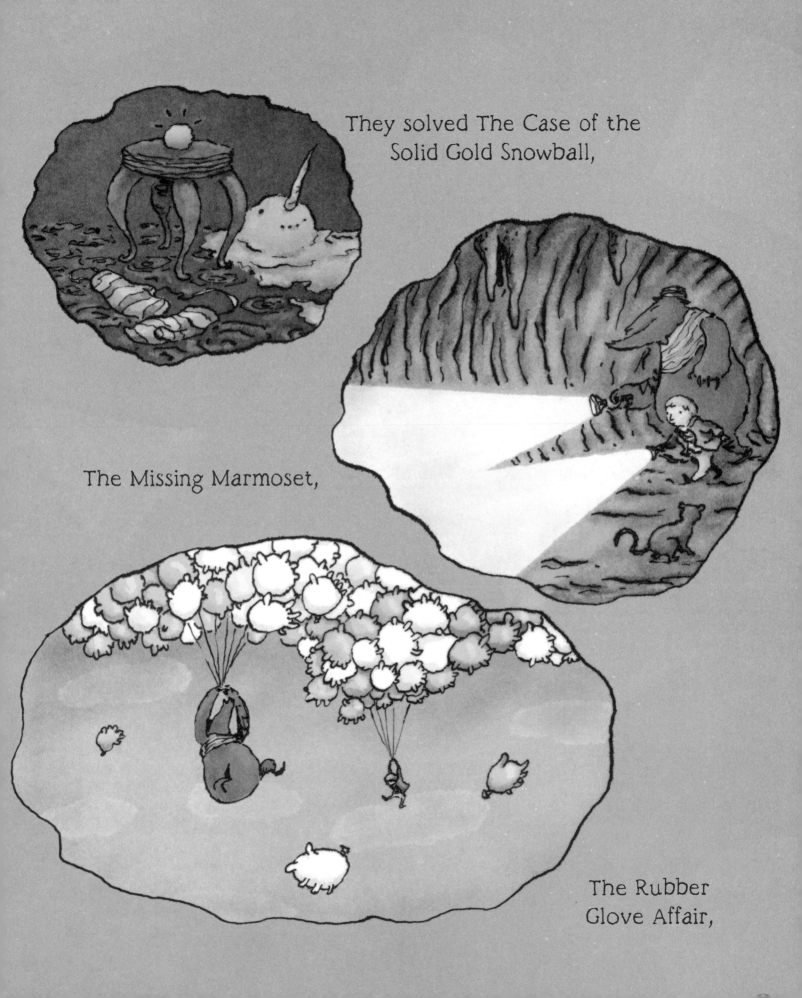

They solved The Case of the
Solid Gold Snowball,

The Missing Marmoset,

The Rubber
Glove Affair,

The Bicycle from Beyond

and The Great Sausage Heist.

They even apprehended their arch nemesis, Professor Hortern Zoar.

Though he later escaped.

"I'M HUNGRY,"

said the
Big Blue Beastie.

"HOLD ON!"

Dexter Bexley invented the biggest, stickiest,
tastiest Yoghurt, Fudge, Banana, Ice-creamy
Beastie Feast ever!

# Really, it was huge!

said Dexter Bexley.

But for once Dexter Bexley
was clean out of ideas.

"I'M CLEAN OUT OF IDEAS,"

said Dexter Bexley.

"I SUPPOSE NOW
YOU'LL **HAVE** TO EAT ME UP."

The Big Blue Beastie bought himself
a very gooey lollipop.

And one for Dexter Bexley.

. . . NOW THAT I'VE FOUND A FRIEND."